LGC ad

'he Attack

\S

Lewis Le, George Scholes, Charlie Brewer

Illustrator: Lewis Le

PROLOGUE: HOW IT ALL BEGAN

Several days ago, Charlie, George and Lewis were fiddling around with their latest invention: The Fire Decker Rocket 3000 (FDR). Crammed with all the latest gadgets and gizmos - including the monstrous Mega Zapper 2.0, which instantly demolished anything in its path - this beastly machine was unstoppable.

In a few days, the three boys were planning to go to space to collect a special rock called moonstone, which could be brewed with Dimendo (a kind of futuristic powder) to make the elixir of life that gives eternal life. In the meantime, Charlie munched on popcorn eagerly.

Lewis wriggled into the shuttle to make some improvements, Charlie and George behind him

Feeling bored, Charlie threw some pieces of popcorn at Lewis.

"Hey! Stop it!" Lewis scowled and lightly pushed Charlie away. Charlie giggled and prodded Lewis back with his plastic cyborg arm from the lab's gift shop.

"Charlie!!!" shouted Lewis while he was losing balance and frantically fell towards the control panel.

"Oops!" he whimpered nervously as he accidentally hit the launch button. All three were silent… disaster struck!!!

CHAPTER ONE: THE RISING OF THE ROCKET

The Fire Decker Rocket 3000 rumbled like a tiger as it began its ascent towards the clouds. George and Lewis stared at Charlie as he looked back at them innocently.

"What have you done!?" they reprimanded Charlie in unison.

"I don't know," Charlie mumbled quietly.

Lewis yelled over the engine's noise, "Get your spacesuit on! We are flying into space!!!"

Awestruck, they looked out into the ever-shrinking roads and cities underneath them which before long just became a dot. They were checking on the rocket and noticed that the tunnalium (fuel for the FDR) meter was running low and they only had half an hour left!

Lewis quickly steered them to a planet not too far away as the tunnalium meter flashed violently in the cramped cabin. It was a panic station! The troublesome trio were running as if there was a lion on the loose, waving their hands aimlessly in the air.

'OH NO!" Charlie desperately wailed into the dark, abysmal and gloomy atmosphere through the window of the spaceship. All he had to keep him company was his two companions, George and Lewis, and his imagination.

The rocket suddenly coughed and spluttered, then bumped heavily onto a dull, forlorn planet. "Oh, dear," moaned George. "The ship has run out of tunnalium!"

Dumbfounded, they got off the spaceship and started to explore the bumpy surface in their beefy spacesuits. The air was bone-chilling, their teeth were chattering even though they had their thermal spacesuits on. They were all still astonished by what had occurred just a few minutes ago. Lewis took out a space compass and they found out where they were - the moon! They were astounded by how far they had come in such a short amount of time.

George scanned the land with his advanced detector; he saw the moonstone that they were looking for in a crater, glowing gold. He reached down and picked it up gingerly from the ground to which it was sticking. They had found the ingredients they needed to make the elixir of life!

"Let's explore more before we go back!" Lewis exclaimed excitedly.

"Help!" Charlie yelled. He was wedged between two large boulders. Lewis' excitement instantly turned to a frown as he looked at Charlie. He, along with George, helped to pull Charlie out.

"Are you alright, Charlie?" asked Lewis.

"Yeah, I'm fine, thanks."

They set off once again exploring. While exploring further, a strange bubbling sound pierced through the silence.

What's that sound?" Lewis hid behind George immediately. They turned around cautiously to see a hoard of slimy, viscous creatures with singular reflective orb eyes rushing towards them at high speed with their clacking talons.

CHAPTER TWO: THE FIGHTING BETWEEN THE ALIENS

Though the aliens were still a long way from them, the boys could smell an unfamiliar stench lingering in the air that was thrown out by the creatures' bodies. The Fertilins advanced towards them rapidly and formed a tight circle around them.

"To the FDR!" cried Charlie and suppressed a shudder. They sped off at high speed away from the aliens towards their rocket. Charlie pulled out three Troop Shoots (a type of laser gun) and handed them to his friends. They were ready for a fight to the death!

George aimed carefully and fired as a burnt alien aroma wafted up their noses.
However, another alien was sneaking up behind them stealthily; menacing, glinting nails at the ready. It launched itself at Lewis who

instinctively whipped around but wasn't quick enough.

"Watch out, Lewis!" Fortunately, George was on the case! While it was in midair, he shot it and it fell to the ground, obliterated.

Then, they turned their attention to the rest of the mob. Charlie tried shooting them all but knew that it wouldn't be enough. He threw his Troop-Shoot to the ground and turned on his unique high tech cyborg arm only used for emergencies. Charlie shot one Fertilin that, because of the Trion Deria (a kind of poison) covering the bullet, it made Charlie be able to control the Fertilin. He decided to make it fight the other aliens.

Charlie shot a few more of them, creating an invincible army against the bloodthirsty beasts. Lewis, George and Charlie returned to the FDR to watch the battle outside. "Hahaha!!!" The three of them rolled on the ground in hysterics watching the aliens fighting each other.

CHAPTER THREE: CHARLIE IS TRAPPED

Poisonous slime oozing off its chest. Limbs sticky as toffee apples. An alien crept around the side of the FDR and loosened the bulletproof window with his dagger-like nails. It climbed in and grabbed Charlie by the ankles. The alien hauled him through the window and clamped its limb over Charlie's mouth.

Charlie writhed in the alien's grip as it carried him over to a nerve-rattling U.F.O. It hauled him in and sat at the controls, flicking and turning switches.

"Charlie!!! No…!!!" shouted George and Lewis. The UFO moved surprisingly fast, so George and Lewis despondently failed to catch up.

Charlie was dragged towards the biggest UFO, where the leader was waiting impatiently. When it saw Charlie, it grinned grotesquely and beckoned him inside the UFO. Inside was an enormous, malicious-looking machine that looked like a torture device! Charlie was horror-struck as he tried to escape the Fertilin's grasp.

"Let me go!!! Let me go!!!" begged Charlie desperately. The Fertilin leaned closer to Charlie's face, its rancid breath making him gag. They put him into a noctilucent glass tube; Charlie was surrounded by a bundle of extraterrestrial lab equipment. The Fertilin was going to experiment on him!

George and Lewis were paralysed by fear. Charlie had been kidnapped! They needed to get him back before it was too late; they needed to think of a plan.

They hatched the most extraordinary, wild, insane plan to get Charlie back. George remembered that he saw the aliens' ships all had forcefields and Lewis glimpsed the firepower that was stored there. They would try to hack into the force field, plant a virus in the system to disable it, and then blow up the entire thing! Charlie would survive because all of their spacesuits were blast-proof and were immune to most lasers.

Whilst walking back to the ship, Lewis asked George, "Our FDR's run out of tunnalium. How do we travel to the Fertilins' base?" Puzzled, they both went into deep thought, silence...

CHAPTER FOUR: CROSSING THE LAVA

As George and Lewis roamed around the moon's surface, searching for materials to fix their ship, Lewis spotted a helical, twinkling tornado on their far right.

"What is that glittering, glamorous thing over there?" Lewis asked inquisitively.

George admonished him, "Watch out! Don't go there. It might be a black hole."

"It doesn't look like a black hole. Let's go and see; we might find something that can help us." Lewis strode towards the tornado, refusing to listen to George.

George trailed after Lewis at a distance until Lewis was a few paces away from the tornado. All of a sudden, an immensely powerful suction pulled him into the mysterious tornado. Instinctively, George sprinted towards Lewis and tried to grab him, but everything happened as quick as lightning. George was sucked in too!

A ringing sound filled their ears as they gasped for air. The force inside the peculiar tornado left them in a dazed dazzle.

After a while, the young inventors thudded onto the surface of a crimson planet that glowed.

"Are you okay, Lewis? Where are we?" George was concerned.

"I'm okay. Are you?" Lewis rummaged in his bag and took out a space compass. The compass blinked then out emerged the name of the planet: S K U L A F A.

When they strode across the scorching sater soil (a type of extremely delicate soil), the two boys saw some small holes in the ground. Under the holes were flaming lakes of lava that hissed violently and spat out sparks of fire. It was shaped like a skull from space with two craters, which looked like eye sockets; lava lakes resembling nostrils and below its nose was a wide opened mouth (an enormous crater) which blew out smoke as if it was angry. Orbiting the planet were gigantic, jagged shards of meteorite that whizzed through the heavens with incredible speed.

George was still contemplating about this place when he was woken from his reverie by a sudden "Argh!"

The soil had fallen under Lewis and he was about to tumble into the lava!

Just as Lewis thought he was going to be incinerated, a large, sturdy limb hauled him out.

"Saved!" he thought, relieved that he was still in one piece. "Thanks, George!"

Lewis then turned around and realised it wasn't George who had saved him.

Lewis squinted at his rescuer and whimpered nervously. The creature gazed at him, as if to say, "Your welcome!", then strolled off.

Lewis's heart was in his mouth. Thousands of questions were racing inside his head. *What was that creature? Why did he help me?* And, most importantly, *Where is George?*

A few minutes later, Lewis breathed a sigh of relief as George sprinted towards him.

I saw this strange creature which looked dangerous, so my first instinct was to run…" babbled George, panting.

"Calm down, George, calm down," Lewis replied coolly. "Did you see what it looked like?"

I didn't see what it looked like; all I know is that it had a pink trunk with a love shaped head, a bit like an elephant! No… an ostrich! No… I don't know!" George shook his head doubtfully.

Don't worry, one of those creatures saved me from falling into the lava," Lewis explained. They are not malignant."

Abruptly, Lewis put a finger to his lips, gesturing for George to be quiet. Whinnying sounds rang through the air as if a choir were singing a harmony. The brave pair gasped in shock. They had never heard or seen this before!

A herd of 'elephants' crawled towards them, swinging their heads to and fro. Their azure-blue, placid eyes reassured the boys that they were benign. They whinnied again; the extraterrestrials were trying to tell them something.

"Luckily, I brought the Alingual-Translator 2.5," grinned Lewis, then swiftly pulled out a portable translator. It read:

Young strangers,
Why are you here?
Do you need any help?

We are here to serve you,
The Blubobs.

"Whoa," whispered George. "Could you tell them if they know where the Fertilins' planet is?"

"I'll try," Lewis muttered.

This time, it read:

The Fertilins have crossed our planet,
and they are heading North of the Galaxy.

Lewis told them Charlie had been captured by the Fertilins. The Blubobs suggested that they could cross the lava to the other side. There, the boys would find a portal.

Our lovely friends,
Let us give you a ride

to the other side.

"Okay. Thanks, Blubob!" said George ecstatically. "Hopefully we can get Charlie back soon!"

"It won't be easy," Lewis warned, recalling the tense fight between them and the Fertilins.

CHAPTER FIVE: BLUBOB RIDING

As the boys bid the other Blubobs farewell, George noticed a little Blubob with beady eyes sitting at his feet. He cautiously bent down to stroke the cute creature and observed how prickly its fiery fur was. *Probably to scare away enemies,* he thought, impressed with the Blubobs' cleverness.

The two boys hopped onto the Blubobs' saddles and levitated over the lava. However, they could feel the intense heat emanating from below.

"Phew! Hold on tight, Lewis, otherwise you might fall into the lava," George was nervous. Lewis grinned.

They finally arrived on the other side, safe and sound. George and Lewis thanked the Blubobs once again and waved them goodbye.

Meanwhile, Charlie was still wriggling and writhing in pain. Tubes clung onto him while monitors flashed and beeped.

LET ME OUT!" Charlie's cries were so loud it startled the aliens. "LET ME OUT!"

The leader was unaffected by the noise and continued to train its eyes on him. Charlie wept until his eyes were dry. He had little hope that George or Lewis could save him now. He knew that, since he was captured, there was going to be higher security. That meant they were going to install force fields around the planet and his box. How could they get in then?

George was scuffing around the dry sater soil until he stubbed his toe against something hard. "Ouuccchh!" he squealed in pain. "That hurts!" He knelt down to examine the ground. The soil that he had scraped away with his foot had started to reveal an old, rusted ring.

"I wonder what this is," George thought to himself, then tugged at it. A narrow trapdoor slowly opened to reveal an old, mossy staircase. He peered down to see steps infinitely winding into darkness. He called Lewis over and together, they walked down the stairs.

CHAPTER SIX: THE SPURIOUS PORTAL

The two were plunged into darkness as the trap door squeaked shut. It was a while before George lit a torch and beckoned Lewis to follow.
They went down a few more steps before George stopped.

"Gosh," huffed George. "Watch out, it's a giant alien spider!"
The hypnotic stare from the spider's kaleidoscopic eyes made them dazed, and it hissed an ear-piercing hiss that the two boys could not bear.

"Agh! Help!" Lewis screamed in agony. "My ears are burning!"
However, George continued to glare at the spider. He had fitted on a pair of special earmuffs just in time and with

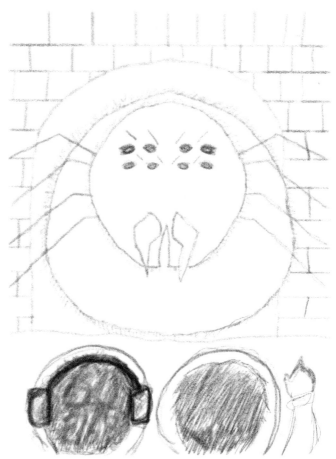

great accuracy began shooting at the spider's devilish red eyes with his trusty Troop Shoot. The spider ceased, lurched backwards and scuttled off.

"Come on! Don't just kneel there!" George snapped. They ran as fast as they could until they reached a dead end.

"Oh gosh!" whimpered Lewis, with his hands still covering his ears. "Do you have any dynamite?".

"Don't think so," George replied, fumbling in his gadget bag. "Nope. there's none left." He eyed Lewis suspiciously.

"I don't have it either," Lewis shrugged.

Swish! An arrow swiftly flew past them, barely skimming George's shoulder. Two more arrows followed and fell on the space rock beneath them. Lewis stared in the direction from which the arrows had come. There were small slits in the walls, and when Lewis chipped them with an Electroknife to make them wider, he found crossbows hidden and loaded with arrows.

"Hey! There are traps everywhere!" Lewis exclaimed angrily as he disarmed the crossbows, then suddenly flinched. A pair of blood-red eyes were glaring at him.

"George! George!" he yelped. "Look!" He pointed in the direction of where the eyes were. George shrugged. "Are you trying to fool me? There's nothing there."

Lewis looked closer and realised that the disembodied eyes were actually lava rock.

"Lewis! Come back!" yelled George, annoyed. There was a WHOOOSSSHHHH noise, and then Lewis was gone.

In front of George was an enormous chalk circle. Lava rock filled the middle, glowing brightly.

"Let's see what happens if I-" George stepped into the circle and disappeared too.

Oh no, he thought to himself as the colours of the spectrum danced around him. *Where will I end up? I hope I can get home.*

He staggered forward and retched, before looking at his surroundings.

It was a portal! George concluded. This unexplored planet was immersed in silence. Craters opened their mouths wide, waiting to trap their prey. The leafless, brobdingnagian stalagmite trees waved their branches, beckoning George to come.

Footprints patterned the dusty ground as he walked by himself. It was a while before George felt a sharp tap on his arm. Instinctively, he turned around and reached for his Troop Shoot. Lewis was there, seeming very concerned.

"Are you okay?" he asked.

"Yeah, I'm fine," George lied, even though he was shaking all over. He then questioned, "Where in the solar system are we?"

"I lost track of where we are," explained Lewis. "Our compass is out of order." George was speechless. Little did they know they were closer to Charlie than they thought..

***

From an Autobiography of a Fertilin

His Majesty has ordered us to get the knives, the samples, the syringes and the laboratory drug. Our Lord announced that he wanted to find out more about the human.

The first step was to inject the drug into him to put him to sleep. Then, we took some blood samples and inserted them into our machine to see the difference between us and the humans. Next, we might need to cut off some of his hair for the tester. We need to scan his body to see what's inside. We need to know this because we plan to overthrow humans and take all their resources. Apparently, a few humans were spotted in one of our UFO's but we're not really that bothered. We have simply the greatest guards.

CHAPTER SEVEN: INTO THE LAB!

Beep… Beep… Lewis heard a vague sound. 'George, did you hear beeping?" He skimmed his eyes across the land.

George paused for a minute, putting his hand behind his ear.

"Yeah! I can hear it. What is it?"

"Let's go and check it out." They cautiously crept to the source of the sound. It got closer and closer until they saw something twinkling. The light flickered from a metallic, cerulean ellipsoid.

"It looks like a U.F.O!" Lewis whispered in awe.

George warned him instantly, "Be careful! There might be something in there!"

Loading their Troop Shoots, the two lads sprung to the hatch and realised it was unlocked. They sneaked into the spacecraft secretly and got ready to fight. They searched through the whole U.F.O but they couldn't find anyone there.

"It could be an abandoned U.F.O," George told Lewis.

"We could function it and pilot it to the aliens' headquarters," exclaimed Lewis, exhilarated.

George cried, "I was thinking that too!"

They strolled to the control room and glimpsed a miscellaneous set of buttons. George, who was interested in U.F.Os, hit a button on the panel.

"Let's see what this does," thought George. They jumped when a loud thump echoed through the U.F.O, then they felt a rumbling vibration.

"The U.F.O's going backwards!" Lewis screamed.

He pulled another lever next to him. The two boys lurched forward. George pressed a silvery, blinking button, which made the U.F.O screech to a halt. Lewis attempted to press nother button and pull a lever simultaneously.

t flew!

Are you ready?" Lewis asked.

Definitely," George said, feeling more

onfident every second.

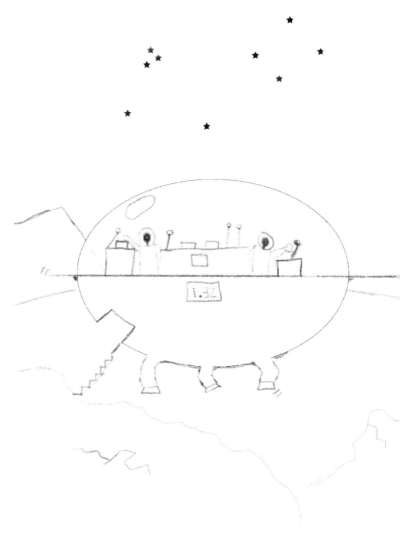

"Blast off!" shouted Lewis. The U.F.O
wobbled towards the Fertilins' planet.
Eventually, they arrived at their destination.

"Oh my gosh!" George gasped. "That was fast!"

There were two guards standing outside the gates, looking fierce. With the butts of the laser guns, Lewis and George knocked them out cold. They tentatively tip-toed over the unconscious aliens and creaked the gate open. Sly as a fox, George borrowed Lewis's tweezers and picked the lock to the hatch of the main UFO while Lewis watched.

"Got to be quick," Lewis muttered hurriedly. "Got to be quick!"

In a few seconds, George picked the lock open and beckoned Lewis to come.

Lewis had an eagle's eye and saw the forcefield, but it was too late to warn George. KABLAM! George smashed straight into it and bounced backwards, his body lifeless.

"GEORGE! NO!" Lewis cried, but George didn't answer. When Lewis checked to see if he was alright, he found George passed out. Tears welled up in Lewis's eyes, but he had to quickly find the way to break through the forcefield before they were discovered by the Fertilins.

Lewis expeditiously examined the forcefield again and saw part of it was very faint. "Aha!" Lewis exclaimed. "There we go!" Lewis went over to the end of the forcefield and eventually found a screen stating:
Forcefield level: weak but controlled.

Then, he started attempting to hack the forcefield, pressing different buttons and pulling levers. After several minutes, the screen said:
Forcefield level: none.

The forcefield shattered like broken glass. Lewis stepped in but then thought about George.

Lewis turned away from the entrance and bent down to George to help him. Suddenly, George stirred, then his eyes opened!

"Wha-what happened?" stammered George.
"You were knocked out by a forcefield. Don't rush next time."
As George got unsteadily to his feet, a laser gun was pressed against Lewis's temple.
George stared, bewildered. How did the Fertilin know they were there?
George searched for his Troop Shoot, but it wasn't there. He glared at the Fertilin.
"What did you do?!?" growled George.
The Fertilin had George's Troop Shoot and pointed at him.

On the other side of the building, the leader gestured to his subordinates to take off Charlie's spacesuit, so that they could inject him and take his blood samples.

"Nooo… Don't they know I need this spacesuit for oxygen supplies?" Charlie thought miserably.

One of the Fertilins examined Charlie's spacesuit and wondered how to open it. It saw the zip behind...

Clung, someone pushed the door open and shoved George and Lewis into the lab to his Master. The leader and his subordinates paused their experiment on Charlie and turned their attention to George and Lewis. It smirked cunningly at them.

In the middle of the lab, a misty cube was jerking up and down while making distorted sounds. The leader imprisoned the boys in the lab, then he went out for dinner and shut the door. Shing!

"Psst! Charlie, is that you?" George whispered in excitement.

Charlie, hearing voices near him, did a strangled yowl.

"Yep, that's him," Lewis smiled. "Now, all we have to do is take him out."

Charlie furiously shook his head. *Don't!* he pleaded in his mind. *Remember the force fields?*

Unfortunately, the duo couldn't see what Charlie was doing. Their eyes moved around and searched for any signs of levers or screens. Lewis spotted a trap door.

"Over here! I found it!" He pointed at the slightly ajar hatch and quietly sidled up to it. With his special screwdriver, he flipped the latch open and crawled inside.

In front of Lewis were millions of microcircuits, which wrapped around Lewis's feet like tentacles. He shook them off, careful not to electrocute himself, then walked further in.

"Wow! How did they get so many circuits?" He wondered.

George took out an Electroknife from his sleeve and told Lewis to stand as far as he could. Then, he threw it into the wires and grinned as sparks scattered around them.

"Run! I blew up the circuits!" George nodded his head at the exit, then charged like a stampede of elephants. The wires were like snakes, angrily spitting electricity. The clamour was followed by a strange beeping from the cube, which was shining a hot red colour.

The coughing boys were knocked off their feet as the canister shattered open, smoke billowing everywhere. Lewis squinted through watery eyes, hoping Charlie had survived.

"Charlie! Charlie, where are you?" he yelled apprehensively.

While the boys were desperately searching for Charlie, they heard him singing the Can Can but they couldn't see him. Descending from the smoke, they found him fox-trotting like a madman, waving his cyborg arm.

"I can't believe you still have the mood for singing," George said sarcastically. "Have you realised we're in hot water?"

"Oh, come on! Give me a moment to celebrate!" replied Charlie jubilantly.

Maybe he's been drugged, Lewis thought.

"Charlie…" George frowned. "Are you okay?"

"Well, I am," Charlie retorted. "I've been in this cage for hours on end!"

George looked at Lewis and shrugged.

A rumbling noise commenced above them. Fraught with worry, they peered up. Tiny cracks in the ceiling had started to merge together until a chunk of metal clattered on the ground. Charlie hopped lightly out of the way as piece after piece tumbled down. They had to get out of this place… and fast!

CHAPTER EIGHT: THE HEADQUARTERS DEMISE

Sirens screeched everywhere as the trio dodged flaming pieces of debris. Grunts and cries mingled in the air while Space Security Dogs - or S.S.Ds - whined in terror. It was chaos!

Charlie, George and Lewis navigated their way through the maze of rubble and dust until they abruptly halted.

'Oh no! How can we get out now?" George shook his head.

However, an idea formed in Lewis's mind. He smiled at Charlie excitedly.

'Charlie! Your cyborg arm!" he cried.

Charlie slowly nodded his head, then smiled too. "Of course! I should have thought of that. I ain't sure if it still works."

He flexed his cyborg arm three times to activate it, then commanded, "Cyber-blast!"

A flash of hyper-energy smashed the chaos to pieces, churning the rocks into pebbles. They repeated this several times before Charlie stumbled forwards.

In a frenzy, they sprinted to their U.F.O which had sent them here previously. The buildings were filled with screams of rage and fear as the boys frantically set up the spacecraft.
"Let's go!" Lewis manned the control panel and launched off back to the moon.

The U.F.O zoomed speedily as a meteor and arrived on the moon, where they had been at the beginning.

"Yes! Over there, our FDR!" Lewis hopped. Their rocket was dented on some spots, but it looked fine. They noticed how comfortable it was inside the shuttle after all that ordeal they had had to endure. George put his feet up while Lewis fiddled with the levers.

What a great adventure, he thought. *I loved it!*

"Launch off!" Lewis yelled into the built-in microphone.

The rocket lifted, then rumbled as it fell quickly back down. Everyone looked dumbfounded.

Lewis nervously tried again. "Launch… off?" It still did not work. Lewis apologised and jumped down to see what had happened to the spaceship. He returned shortly after and reported to his companions. Everyone listened on with grim expressions.

"First thing, a Fertilin was in our engine, hammering at it, and now the engine's broken. Another thing-" he paused dramatically- "Don't you remember that there is no Gunnalium on the moon. We have to return to Earth as soon as possible."

George gasped and shuddered. "How will we ever get back to Earth, then?"

Lewis turned to George and nodded, sadness washed on his face.

CHAPTER NINE: BACK ON EARTH

"What should we do?!" Charlie shrieked, his breath getting shallower every minute.

"Hush, I'm trying to think," Lewis put on his blast-proof helmet. "I'm going down to try…" before he could finish his sentence, Lewis darted towards the engine room.

A few hours later, Lewis returned to his crew dirty and tired but with his face gleeful with relief. Their poor spacecraft was mended! The engine gradually spluttered back to life and growled like a lion. The capsule lifted, then accelerated.

"How did it suddenly work again?" George asked.

They peered through the window to see a Fertilin waving at them. George waved back to thank the kind extraterrestrial for helping them to fix their spacecraft.

"It was this kind Fertilin who repaired it for us!"

"It's incredible! Aliens have much more advanced technology than us!" Charlie rushed towards the window and smiled at the Fertilin.

"Do you know that guy, Charlie?" Lewis asked.

"Yep. I met him a few times when I was in my 'little box'. He was very nice, and always secretly gave me their cuisines such as roast mayum." Charlie gazed up at the ceiling. "Mayum was the national snack. It was made from small, round slabs of chewy rock. It was left to soak in a salty water source. You suck as hard as you can on the rock, which makes it release a scrumptious taste." He licked his lips longingly. "I'll never forget that moment."

Charlie went into silence when thinking of how they could pay back this extraterrestrial pal.

Exhaustion had made Lewis light-headed, he blinked his eyes and stretched arms behind his head. "Come on. We're nearly there!"
Lewis was correct. The distinctive shape of Earth was sailing closer... closer...

***

The kind Fertilin was in jail. Darkness surrounded him, forcing him onto his knees. However, he was content that the trio had escaped. He had hatched a plan with some other rebels to overthrow their leader. Everything would be okay...
Would it not?

CHAPTER TEN: HOME SWEET HOME

The boys landed on earth safe and sound, they couldn't wait to rush home and see their family.

Charlie felt the light breeze of England and the saccharine smell of the sweet shop near him. It felt too good to be back home. Everyone - including his sister - had patted him on the back, saying he had shot up in size. It was true; zero gravity had elongated the boys' spines, making them taller.

Meanwhile, Lewis's family made a space-themed cake to celebrate his return to Earth. They delivered a fair share to each of the families.

George, however, was having the best time of all; he was enrolled in an advanced degree in science and was invited to join a significant project by the Worldwide Inventors Organisation.

One week later, Lewis arrived at George's house and rang the doorbell. Ding dong! George answered the door. "Hey, Lewis! What's up?"

"I got a Galaxy bar," Lewis panted. "And you'll never guess what came with it."

"What?" George inquired.

Lewis had a shine in his eye as he spoke. "A clue to £5,000,000 worth of emeralds."

"That's amazing!" George marvelled aloud. "£5,000,000,000 worth of emeralds- that's utterly amazing."

They had set off to tell Charlie the clue they had found in the wrapper. They breathed life into the next adventure; they must find the emeralds before anyone else did.

THE END

Join Lewis, George and Charlie on the next
stage in the LGC adventures.

Find

THE GALAXY CRUMBLES

Can the boys find the emeralds?

Printed in Great Britain
by Amazon